ALBERT THE FIX-IT MAN

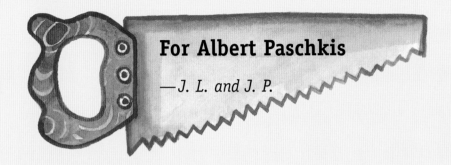

For Albert Paschkis

—J. L. and J. P.

Published by
PEACHTREE PUBLISHERS
1700 Chattahoochee Avenue
Atlanta, Georgia 30318-2112
www.peachtree-online.com

Book and cover design by Julie Paschkis and Loraine M. Joyner
Illustrations created in watercolor on 100% rag archival watercolor paper. Title is handlettered. Text is typeset in International Typeface Corporation's Officina Serif.

Printed in April 2018 by RR Donnelley & Sons in China
10 9 8 7 6 5 4 (hardcover)
10 9 8 7 6 5 4 (trade paperback)

HC ISBN: 978-1-56145-433-4
PB ISBN: 978-1-56145-830-1

Library of Congress Cataloging-in-Publication Data

Lord, Janet.
Albert the Fix-it Man / written by Janet Lord ; illustrated by Julie Paschkis.— 1st ed.
p. cm.
Summary: A cheerful repairman fixes squeaky doors, leaky roofs, and crumbling fences for his neighbors, who return the kindness when he catches a terrible cold.
ISBN 978-1-56145-433-4
[1. Repairing—Fiction. 2. Kindness—Fiction. 3. Community life—Fiction.] I. Paschkis, Julie, ill. II. Title.
PZ7.L8774Al 2007
[E]—dc22
2007029465

ALBERT THE FIX-IT MAN

Story by Janet Lord   Pictures by Julie Paschkis

Ω
PEACHTREE
ATLANTA

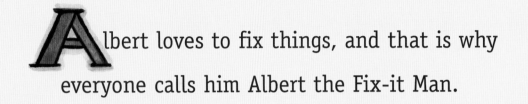lbert loves to fix things, and that is why
everyone calls him Albert the Fix-it Man.

Albert's always on the lookout for

things to fix.

Here's a rusty hinge.

Albert oils it.

The roof is leaky. Albert climbs
up and hammers on a new shingle.
The house is snug and dry again.

Next door, Auntie Miller's goat jumps into

her garden and starts to eat the beans.

Albert races to patch the fence.

Now Auntie Miller's beans will be safe.

The neighbors know that Albert can fix anything,

so they often ask for his help.

Albert is never too busy. Albert is never too tired.

Albert the Fix-it Man hoists up Mr. Jensen's old

green truck and repairs the motor.

Soon it's running almost as good as new.

Albert ties up Akiko's clothesline between two stout apple trees so her sheets can dry in the sun and wind.

Now they'll smell fresh and clean.

Amy visits Mrs. Peabody and sets out tea and muffins. Somehow the blue-striped cup slips and breaks. Mrs. Peabody almost throws it away.

"Stop!" says Albert the Fix-it Man. "You don't need to do that."

He glues the two parts together. "When the glue dries, it will be fine."

Mrs. Peabody pours Albert a cup of tea, and Amy offers him a muffin.

He suddenly stops to listen.

A *drip-drip-drip* noise is coming from the kitchen.

He grabs his toolbox and goes inside to investigate.

It only takes Albert a few minutes to fix the leaky faucet.

"Wow," says Mrs. Peabody. "You take care of everything!"

Many things have been fixed.
It has been a good day and now
it's time to rest.

After a bowl of
his favorite cereal,
Albert the Fix-it Man
hops into bed,
closes his eyes,
and goes to sleep.

He dreams about broken bicycles and loose floorboards.

The next morning Albert feels dizzy and his bones ache. He has a terrible cold.

Albert can't even manage to get out of bed.

Sam delivers the paper and

pokes his head in the door.

Albert can barely croak hello.

Sam tells everyone
on his paper route that
Albert the Fix-it Man
is not feeling well.

When Auntie Miller hears the news,
she cooks Albert a big pot of green beans
to help him get better.

Akiko bakes an apple pie and sprinkles it with cinnamon as a get-well treat for Albert. She covers it with a red-checkered cloth.

Mrs. Peabody pours fresh water
and brews a steaming pot of minty tea.

Amy places it on a tray
next to the blue-striped cup.

Mr. Jensen drives everybody
over to Albert the Fix-it Man's
house in his old green truck.

"Don't hit any big bumps!"
says Amy.

At Albert's house they knock quietly in case
the Fix-it Man is sleeping.

Who can that be? wonders Albert. "Come in,"
he calls out weakly.

Albert starts to feel better the moment he sees
all of his friends. After a meal of fresh beans,
hot apple pie, and minty tea, he feels even better.

Everyone leaves, and Albert pulls the covers back up to his chin. He's full to the brim, and he knows he is on the mend.

Just before he drifts off to sleep, Albert the Fix-it Man notices that the clock is making a peculiar noise.

Good, he thinks. *Something for me to fix first thing in the morning.*